W9-AMS-540

Sadie's Almost Marvelous Menorah

For Sarah and Emma with love —J.K.
For Don, with love—J.F.

Kar-Ben Publishing
A division of Lerner Publishing Group, Inc.
241 First Avenue North
Minneapolis, MN 55401 U.S.A.

Website address: www.lernerbooks.com

Library of Congress Cataloging-in-Publication Data

Korngold, Jamie S.
   Sadie's almost marvelous menorah / by Jamie Korngold ; illustrated by Julie Fortenberry.
        p.   cm.
      Summary: A little girl breaks her handmade Hanukkah menorah but learns that, even broken, it can still have a role to play in the holiday celebration.
      ISBN 978-0-7613-6493-1 (lib. bdg. : alk. paper)
      [1. Hanukkah—Fiction. 2. Menorah—Fiction.] I. Fortenberry, Julie, 1956— ill.
   II. Title.
   PZ7.K83749Sack 2012
   [E]—dc23   2011029042

Manufactured in the United States of America
1 – PP – 7/15/11

Sadie's Almost Marvelous Menorah

By Jamie Korngold

illustrated by Julie Fortenberry

KAR-BEN
PUBLISHING

Sadie loved school.

She loved the Hebrew songs the children sang during music,

the wooden play sink in the kitchen corner, and...

the reading nook with its comfy chairs and colorful books.

She loved the boys and girls in her class and she especially loved her teacher, Morah Rachel.

One Monday morning at circle time, Morah Rachel asked the class, "Can you guess what holiday starts this week?"

All the children chimed in at once, "Hanukkah!"

Sadie loved Hanukkah. She loved to spin dreidels,

and to eat potato latkes with applesauce.

Most of all, she loved to help Mommy and
Daddy light their Hanukkah menorahs.

Morah Rachel said, "This week we are going to make our own menorahs."

"How exciting!" thought Sadie. "My very own Hanukkah menorah!"
Sadie couldn't wait to start.

On Tuesday, Morah Rachel brought out big blocks of clay for each child. The children kneaded, rolled, and shaped their menorahs. Sadie used a pencil to poke holes in the clay to hold eight candles. Then she rolled a small ball of clay, put one more hole in it, and attached it to the top. This was for the shammash, the candle used to light all the others.

On Wednesday, Morah Rachel brought out different colors of paint. There was purple, blue, red, orange, green, yellow, and pink. The children put on their smocks and began to paint. They speckled and spotted and striped their menorahs. Sadie painted hers pink with blue squiggles.

On Thursday, Morah Rachel taught the children the Hanukkah blessings and they all sang them together.

On Friday, Sadie ran all the way to school, because today she would take home her pink and blue menorah. All morning she imagined how it would look on the window sill in the living room.

At pick-up time, Sadie waited for her mommy to arrive. As soon as she saw her, she started to run. But in her excitement, she tripped and fell, and the menorah flew out of her arms.

Sadie burst into tears and ran across the room into her mother's arms. "Mommy, Mommy! I dropped my menorah and it broke into a million, zillion pieces!"

Sadie's mother hugged her and said, "Let's see if we can pick them up and glue them back together." But even as she spoke, her mother could see that the shattered pieces were too small.

There were pieces of Sadie's menorah in the dress up corner and pieces in the block corner. There were pieces under the snack table and pieces under the easel. Silently, the children began to help gather them. Morah Rachel placed all the pieces in a small plastic bag.

As they left the classroom , Sadie noticed something near the door.
"Look, it's the shammash," she said. "And it's not broken."
"Sadie, this is an extra special shammash," her mother said, "and
I think we can find an extra special job for it.

"You know that when we light the menorah, we use the shammash to light all the other candles. But how do we light the shammash? That can be the job for your shammash. We'll call it **Sadie's Super Shammash!**"

Sadie picked up her little pink shammash and cradled it ever so carefully in her hands.

That night Sadie, her brother Ori, her parents, and grandparents gathered to light the first Hanukkah candle. They had decorated the house with drawings of dreidels, menorahs, and Stars of David. The table was covered with latkes, doughnuts, and Hanukkah gelt. On the window sill stood four Hanukkah menorahs, waiting to be lit. Right in the middle was Sadie's little pink and blue Super Shammash.

Sadie put a candle in her Super Shammash, and Daddy helped her light it. Then carefully she used it to light the shammash on all four menorahs.

And in Sadie's family, that is how the Hanukkah menorahs are lit, even today.

Candle Blessings

בָּרוּךְ אַתָּה יְיָ אֱלֹהֵינוּ מֶלֶךְ הָעוֹלָם אֲשֶׁר קִדְשָׁנוּ בְּמִצְוֹתָיו וְצִוָּנוּ לְהַדְלִק נֵר שֶׁל חֲנֻכָּה.

Baruch Atah Adonai Eloheinu melech ha'olam asher kideshanu b'mitzvotav v'tzivanu l'hadlik ner shel Hanukkah.

We praise you, Adonai our God, Ruler of the World, who makes us holy by Your mitzvot and commands us to light the Hanukkah candles.

בָּרוּךְ אַתָּה יְיָ אֱלֹהֵינוּ מֶלֶךְ הָעוֹלָם שֶׁעָשָׂה נִסִּים לַאֲבוֹתֵינוּ בַּיָּמִים הָהֵם בַּזְּמַן הַזֶּה.

Baruch Atah Adonai Eloheinu melech ha'olam she'asah nisim la'avoteinu bayamim hahem baz'man hazeh.

We praise you, Adonai our God, Ruler of the World, who made miracles for our ancestors in those days.

בָּרוּךְ אַתָּה יְיָ אֱלֹהֵינוּ מֶלֶךְ הָעוֹלָם שֶׁהֶחֱיָנוּ וְקִיְּמָנוּ וְהִגִּיעָנוּ לַזְּמַן הַזֶּה.

Baruch Atah Adonai Eloheinu melech ha'olam shehecheyanu, v'kiyemanu, v'higianu, lazman hazeh.

We praise you, Adonai our God, Ruler of the World, who has kept us alie and well so that we can celebrate this special time.

About the Author

Rabbi Jamie S. Korngold, who received ordination from the Hebrew Union College-Jewish Institute of Religion, is the founder and spiritual leader of the Adventure Rabbi Program. She has competed in marathons, national ski competitions, and rode her bike across the U.S. at age 16. She has worked as a street musician in Japan and as a cook on a boat in Alaska. Rabbi Korngold is the author of "Sadie's Sukkah Breakfast" and "Sadie and the Big Mountain" (Kar-Ben), "God in the Wilderness" (Doubleday), and "The God Upgrade" (Jewish Lights). She lives in Boulder, Colorado with her husband and two daughters..

About the Illustrator

Julie Fortenberry is an abstract painter and a children's book illustrator. She has a Master's Degree in Fine Arts from Hunter College in New York. Her illustrations have appeared in "Highlights High Five," "Ladybug," and "Babybug" Magazines. Her children's books include "Sadie's Sukkah Breakfast" and "Sadie and the Big Mountain" (Kar-Ben) and "Pippa at the Parade" (Boyds Mills Press). She lives in Westchester County, New York.